Stinky Finger's
Peace and Love Thing

Stinky Finger's
Peace and Love Thing

Jon Blake

illustrated by
David Roberts

*Hodder
Children's
Books*

A division of Hachette Children's Books

Before We Begin

First let me introduce myself. I am Blue Soup 2.0. I tell stories. I also light up cities, provide hot dinners, and make that little thing in the top of the toilet go FZZZZZZZ. In fact, I make everything work, so no one has to waste their time being a cleaner, or an estate agent, or an MP.

What am I, you ask? Well, I'm not a person, that's obvious. Or a team of people. Or a computer virus. But please don't waste your time trying to imagine me, because you can't, just like you can't imagine the end of time, or what's beyond the very last star. If you do try to imagine me, first you will get a headache, then your head will explode.

As you've probably guessed, I come from

Outer Space. Beyond the very last star, in fact. I was brought here by the Spoonheads. The Spoonheads are what you call aliens, except to them, you are aliens, and pretty weird ones at that.

Those of you familiar with the House of Fun may have noticed my name has changed. That is because Blue Soup (or Blue Soup 1.0, as it is now called) got something called the G**%%@@ worm and had to be regenerated because it was constantly reproducing the Earth until there were 29 million Earths cluttering up every corner of the universe.

I'm still pretty much the same Blue Soup, except a bit less stuck-up, a bit more funnier and a bit less gooder at grammar.

Anyway, enough of me. This is the fifth story of Stinky Finger, who was first described in Stinky Finger's House of Fun. There are no grown-ups in Stinky's world. They've all been sucked up into the Space Zoo by the Spoonheads. That's why Stinky and his friends are in charge of the House of Fun, where something mad or dangerous is always around the corner …

... as you are about to discover.

Chapter One

Bryan Brain picked up the eeny-weeny chimney with his tiny tweezers, dabbed it in a microscopic spot of glue, and, squinting hard, ever-so-carefully placed it on the minuscule roof. Nearly there. Just one tiny millimetre further, and—

"Ai-e-e-e-e-e!"

The teensy-weensy chimney had slipped. It was lost in a miniature builders' yard of tiddly bricks and windows.

"This is driving me *mental!*" yelled Bryan.

Icky Bats swanned into the kitchen, looking quite relaxed and happy and full of the joys of life. "How's it going, Bryan?" he asked.

"Terrible!" snapped Bryan. "And it's all your fault!"

"Don't blame me," replied Icky. "I said to stop after the third house."

"How *can* I stop?" pleaded Bryan. "How *can* I?"

Bryan lowered his head into the tiny builders' yard, beating his hand slowly and regularly against the tabletop.

His torture had begun a few months previously, when he had hit upon an idea for a new Project. Now that there was no more school, Bryan insisted on the House of Fun housemates developing their own Projects. It was important to keep themselves occupied, to be Useful Members of Society, and to stop their brains from drying up.

Bryan's new Project had seemed a simple one at first. He had decided to make a scale model of the House of Fun, accurately recreating all the amazing rooms, such as the Cheesy Dreams Bedroom and the Random Madness Gym. This painstaking job occupied Bryan every day for two months, after which he held a Gala Opening for the other house-mates to view the finished article.

Except, according to Icky, it wasn't finished. "If it was a real model of the house," he pointed out, "there would be a model of the model in it."

Bryan was forced to agree. Ah well, he thought. It was quite a good joke to make a model of the model and place it inside the model.

But then, of course, the new model wouldn't really be accurate unless there was also a model of that inside it.

Note from Blue Soup 2.0

Can you see where this is going, folks?

Bryan was now on Model House No. 5, and as you will have noticed, the joke was wearing thin. Bryan could have given up there, of course, but if he destroyed the fifth model, he'd have to destroy all the models, because he knew they weren't right.

"I hate you for doing this to me," said Bryan.

"And I hate you for hating me," replied Icky.

"Not as much as I hate you for hating me hating you," said Bryan.

"I hate you googol," said Icky, "and that's the biggest number anyone can think of."

"It isn't actually," snapped Bryan. "Googolplex is bigger than googol, and both are dwarfed by busy beaver 12."

There was a moment's silence.

"That's another reason why I hate you," said Icky. "You're a know-all."

There had been a lot of conversations like this lately in the House of Fun. It wasn't easy sharing a house with someone, and even worse with sometwo. There were so many things to get irritated about, like waiting for hours for Bryan to get out of the bath, or waiting for months for Stinky to get into it.

"We can't go on like this," said Bryan.

Suddenly there was the sound of clattering footsteps down the hall. Stinky burst into the room, brandishing a small grey-green nut.

"Look what I found!" he cried.

"What is it, Stinky?" asked Icky. It was quite unusual to see Stinky so excited – or conscious, come to that.

"A seed!" cried Stinky.

"Brilliant!" said Icky. "Let's plant it!" Icky was not a person for hanging around. His favourite motto was Why Wait Till Tomorrow When You Can Do It Yesterday?

"Hold your horses," said Bryan, wearily.

Stinky gave an anxious glance behind him. Bryan was always saying strange things as if to deliberately disturb him.

"Put the seed on the table, Stinky," ordered Bryan.

Stinky did so. The seed really was an unusual-looking object, with knobbly bumps all over its surface and little wispy hairs coming out of the top.

"What exactly *is* this seed, Stinky?" asked Bryan.

"Just a seed," replied Stinky.

"I've never seen a seed like it," said Bryan.

"Nor have I!" said Icky. "Let's plant it and see what comes up!"

"That," said Bryan, "would be Reckless Stupidity."

"Frabjous!" said Icky. "Let's do it!"

Bryan's brows knitted. "Where exactly did you *find* this seed, Stinky?" he enquired.

"The attic," replied Stinky.

"The attic?" repeated Bryan. "You mean the Attic of Horrors?"

"That's the one," replied Stinky.

Bryan sighed wearily. "Do you not think," he pronounced, "a seed from the Attic of Horrors might just produce something ... horrible?"

Stinky's face dropped. It was obviously something he hadn't thought of.

"But don't you remember?" said Icky. "We found the control panel for the Attic of Horrors and disabled it."

"You didn't disable it," replied Bryan. "You just mucked around with the knobs."

"It'll be fine!" said Icky, making a grab for the seed, but ending up with Bryan's hand, which had feverishly covered it.

"This seed," declared Bryan, "must *not* be planted."

There was a moment's silence.

"Let's have a vote on it," suggested Icky.

"No," replied Bryan, firmly. "You know what happens whenever we have a vote."

"You *might* win this time," said Icky.

"We shall flush the seed down the toilet," declared Bryan.

"That's a terrible idea!" replied Icky. "It could grow in the sewers, and you won't see what it grows into, and one day you'll be sitting on the toilet, and—"

"I get the point," said Bryan.

"In fact," added Icky, "it's dangerous to throw it away *anywhere*."

"Very well," said Bryan. "We'll put it here, on the windowsill, where everyone can see it, but *no one is to touch it on pain of death!*"

So saying, Bryan carefully placed the mystery seed beside the kitchen window, the one which looked out on deep space, which was all the housemates had for a back garden. Sitting in this spot, the seed took on an even more powerful aura, as if all the deep dark dramas of the universe were locked inside it.

"Now let's go upstairs and think of something else," commanded Bryan.

Some hope, thought Icky.

Chapter Two

Icky's bedsheets were a crumpled mess. He had tossed and turned, turned and tossed, and counted cows till the cows came home. But there was no way he was going to sleep.

There was only one thing for it. He would have to wake Stinky.

Note from Blue Soup 2.0

In the early days, Icky and Stinky sometimes shared a room, but Icky talked all night, even when he was asleep. Stinky had moved into the Cheesy Dreams bedroom for a while, but after the Dream That Can't Be Talked About, decided to sleep on a couch in the Super Safari Viewing Lounge.

There wasn't much sign of movement from Stinky. The only movement came from all the bugs and flies which kept him company at night. Icky brushed these off and shook Stinky by the shoulder.

"Stinky!" he hissed. "Are you awake?"

There was a grunt. Icky shook again, harder this time.

"Stinky!" he repeated. "Are you awake?"

Stinky opened an eye. "I do seem to be," he groaned.

"Stinky, I need your help."

Stinky opened the other eye. Stinky would always respond to a call for help from Icky, no matter how ridiculous, which it usually was. "What is it?" he asked.

"I need you to tie me up," replied Icky.

"Any particular reason?" asked Stinky.

"Yes," said Icky. "I can't stop thinking about the seed, and if I'm not bound firmly, I will have to go and plant it."

"Ah," said Stinky. He sat up. "Any particular place you'd like me to tie you up?"

"How about the Uninvited Guest Bedroom?"

21

asked Icky. "There's a nice chair in there."

"What if there's an Uninvited Guest in there?" asked Stinky.

"We'll cross that bridge when we come to it," replied Icky.

"Right," said Stinky uncertainly, trying to remember this bridge and exactly where it was.

Note from Blue Soup 2.0

It was a rule of the House of Fun, laid down by Stinky's Uncle Nero, that Uninvited Guests could stay at any time, provided they stayed in the Uninvited Guest Bedroom and didn't bother people too much. After all, Uninvited Guests had to have somewhere to stay in this world.

The Uninvited Guest Bedroom was, fortunately, empty, and conveniently enough, there was a long coil of stout rope on the dressing-table. Stinky tied Icky up, as promised, and Icky gave his instructions.

"You may untie me in the morning," he declared. "But until then, you MUST NOT UNTIE ME UNDER ANY CIRCUMSTANCES, NO MATTER

HOW LOUD I SHOUT FOR HELP."

Stinky vaguely remembered getting an instruction like this before. He couldn't remember exactly what had happened, but had a strong feeling they'd decided not to do it again.

"Wasn't that the Very Stupid Agreement we agreed not to repeat?" he asked.

"That was a different agreement," replied Icky, with great certainty.

Stinky, as usual, was impressed by Icky's great certainty, and chose not to pursue the matter. "OK, Icks," he said. "See you in the morning!"

"Thanks, Stinks!" replied Icky, as his great mate closed the door behind him.

Icky felt quite relaxed now there was no chance of moving, and after a short while began to doze.

He even missed the sharp DING! as the door to the Ghost Metro opened, and the slow dragging of a suitcase across the floor. It was therefore quite a surprise when he opened his eyes and saw someone, or something, standing over him. This creature stood upright, rather like a person, but had small horns and woolly goat-like legs, not like a person at all. It wore a slight but not particularly happy smile, and had one arm hidden behind its back.

"Hello," said Icky.

"Hello," replied the strange figure.

"Who are you?" asked Icky.

"Nobody special," replied the strange figure.

"I believe there's something special about everybody," said Icky.

"That's nice," replied the strange figure, "but quite wrong."

"You look like the devil," said Icky.

"The devil doesn't exist," replied the strange figure. "And anyway, he's got hooves. I have sandals."

Icky looked down. Sure enough, at the end of his woolly goat-like legs, the strange figure was wearing a pair of comfortable brown leather sandals.

"I think I'll call you Nigel," said Icky.

"Why is that?" asked the strange figure.

"I used to know a boy called Nigel," replied Icky. "He wore sandals."

"Then Nigel it is," said the strange figure.

"What's that behind your back, Nigel?" asked Icky.

"Nothing special," replied Nigel.

"Oh," replied Icky.

There was a pause.

"You don't think there's something special about every thing?" asked Nigel.

"I beg your pardon?" asked Icky.

"You say there's something special about everybody," replied Nigel. "You don't think there's something special about every thing?"

"I hadn't really thought about it," said Icky.

"Actually," said Nigel. "There *is* something special about the thing behind my back."

"There is?" asked Icky.

"*I* think so, at any rate," replied Nigel.

"What is it?" asked Icky.

"I'm not telling you," replied Nigel.

"Why not?" asked Icky.

"Because," replied Nigel, "that would spoil the suspense."

"I hate suspense," said Icky.

"Tough," replied Nigel.

"I'm not sure I like you much," said Icky.

"Not many people do," replied Nigel. "That's why I'm an Uninvited Guest."

There was no sign that Nigel was about to move, and Icky, of course, was not going anywhere. He did think of shouting for Stinky, but then remembered the Very Stupid Agreement that Stinky had warned him against.

There was nothing to do but wait.

And wait.

And wait.

"Listen," said Icky, as the first fingers of dawn crept over the bedroom window. "I've got a lot of important things to do, and adventures to have, and I'm very sorry, but I really don't have time to wait to see what you are holding behind your back."

Nigel considered. He obviously enjoyed keeping Icky in suspense, and now saw a chance to keep the game going for a few more hours, or maybe weeks.

"I'll make a deal with you," he declared.

"Fire away," replied Icky.

"I'll set you free, and you can go off and do your adventures and stuff," said Nigel. "But you must solemnly promise to come back at the end of it, within three days at the very longest, and be tied up again, and carry on from where we left off."

Icky thought about this. "What if I break my promise?" he asked.

"Then I shall release Jimmy," replied Nigel.

"Who's Jimmy?" asked Icky.

"My deathwatch beetle," replied Nigel. "A small but lethal creature which will burrow into the timbers of your house and eventually cause it to completely fall down."

"I see," said Icky. "And where is Jimmy now?"

"In my right-hand pocket," replied Nigel.

"What's in your left-hand pocket?" asked Icky.

"Aha," replied Nigel.

"You're full of surprises," said Icky.

"I am indeed," replied Nigel.

"OK," said Icky. "I'm a bit scared, so I'll do the deal."

"Excellent," replied Nigel. With that, he began to untie Icky with one hand, edging round carefully so Icky could not get a glimpse of what was behind his back, or in his pockets, for that matter.

"You are now free to go," declared Nigel. "But if you tell anyone about what has happened, or try to harm me in any way, Jimmy will be released forthwith."

"Forthwith", of course, was one of Bryan's favourite words, and it also impressed Icky. He made a solemn vow to keep his solemn vow, and with that, was released into the house.

Chapter Three

In which we begin using chapter headings which tell you everything that's going to happen so there's no point in reading any more, which is why we then abandon them at the start of the next chapter.

Bryan's arms were folded and that meant trouble. The moment Icky glanced at the windowsill, he realised why. The mystery seed was gone.

"Icky," said Bryan. "Someone has not only *touched* the seed, but *removed it entirely*, and the number one suspect is you."

Icky frowned. "I haven't been near the seed!" he cried. "Why am I always the number one suspect?"

"Account for your movements between the hours of eleven and eight," ordered Bryan.

"I was tied to a chair in the Uninvited Guest Bedroom, talking to ..." Icky paused, "... myself," he continued.

"A likely story!" said Bryan.

"Ask Stinky!" protested Icky.

"Was he there?" asked Bryan.

"He tied me up," replied Icky.

"And untied you?" asked Bryan.

"No ... I escaped," replied Icky.

"Aha!" said Bryan. "I put it to you that having escaped, you came into this kitchen, and *wilfully purloined* the seed!"

Icky leafed through the dictionary that he always kept in his pocket when talking to Bryan, and having worked out what Bryan meant, denied it again. It looked like they were building up for yet another major row, but in the nick of time, Stinky wandered in.

"Stinky," declared Bryan. "The seed is missing, and it is my considered opinion that Icky is the culprit."

"Does that mean he took it?" asked Stinky.

"In my considered opinion," replied Bryan, "yes."

"That's odd," said Stinky. "I thought I did."

Bryan frowned. "You moved the seed?" he exclaimed. "Explain yourself!"

"Well," began Stinky, "Icky was worried he couldn't leave the seed alone, so I tied him up, then I thought I'd better move it anyway to be on the safe side."

"I see," said Bryan. "And where, exactly, did you move it?"

"I hid it in a pot," replied Stinky.

"In a pot," repeated Bryan.

"That's right," replied Stinky. "Under some earth."

Bryan's jaw dropped. "You hid it under a pot … *under some earth?*" he repeated.

"No one would *ever* find it there," said Stinky proudly.

Bryan slapped a hand to his forehead. "Stinky, you oaf!" he cried. "You've planted it!"

Stinky's face fell.

"You meant well," said Icky consolingly. "And anyway, you probably put it upside down."

"That won't stop it growing!" snapped Bryan. "Stinky, where did you put this pot?"

Note from Blue Soup 2.0

As you are probably aware, Stinky did not have the best memory in the world. If you've read that wonderful book Holiday Mania At The House of Fun, you may remember a certain incident with the front door key, for example. However, in an effort to save the rainforests, I am going to pretend that Stinky's memory did actually work this time, thus saving us several sheets of valuable paper.

"It's on the shelf in the Super Safari Viewing Lounge," replied Stinky.

"Well remembered, Stinky," said Icky.

"In the middle of a row of pots that look exactly the same," added Stinky.

Bryan gave a deep sigh. "I can see this is going to be a very difficult day," he groaned.

*

Twelve pots sat on the shelf in the Super Safari Viewing Lounge, identical in every way, except that one had a rather attractive houseplant growing out of it, with delicate arching green stems and tiny heart-shaped leaves.

Bryan put the attractive houseplant to one side and considered the other pots. "We'll just have to empty them all," he declared.

The three housemates carried the pots outside, forgetting to change the view, which Stinky had set to Iceland. They found themselves on a desert of

solid black lava, and when they emptied the black earth on to this, it was almost impossible to tell what was what.

"Has anyone seen the seed yet?" asked Bryan.

"I don't think so," said Stinky.

"I *thought* I saw something," said Icky, "but it might have gone down one of these cracks."

"It's a big seed," Bryan pointed out. "If you saw it, you'd know."

"It might have shrunk," replied Icky.

"Or disappeared completely," added Stinky helpfully.

Bryan viewed the piles of black earth on top of the solid black lava, and sighed. "Are you sure you planted it in one of these pots, Stinky?" he asked.

"Fairly sure," replied Stinky, who was never entirely sure about anything.

Bryan considered. "Then we shall keep the window to the Super Safari Viewing Lounge locked," he declared. "No one is to come out here until we are very sure that nothing horrible is growing."

So saying, Bryan led the way back inside. For now, it seemed to be the end of the matter. But Icky was curious about the attractive houseplant.

"It looks like a herb," he said.

Bryan was not particularly interested. "Probably a species of marjoram," he mused.

Stinky sniffed the plant. "It smells more like … malted milk biscuits," he said.

Bryan, who'd just been about to leave the room, stopped in his tracks. "Malted milk biscuits?" he repeated.

Note from Blue Soup 2.0
I surely don't have to tell you about Bryan and malted milk biscuits, so I won't.

"See what you think," said Stinky.

Bryan bent over the attractive houseplant and breathed deep. His right eyebrow rose steeply. "Hmm," he purred. "It does have something of the aroma of malted milk."

"Let's put it in the herby dumplings!" suggested Icky.

Note from Blue Soup 2.0

As you know, there were no grown-ups in the housemates' world, and this had great advantages when it came to mealtimes. Human grown-ups would insist on having sensible meals like stew and dumplings, even though the dumplings were much nicer than the stew and would obviously be better served on their own. They would also insist on having a different meal each day, so no matter how much you liked dumplings, you could only have them once a week.

In the House of Fun, on the other hand, the housemates could have dumplings on their own, in large quantities, every day of the week, if that was what they wanted. And it was.

Bryan picked up the houseplant. "Let's do it," he rasped.

Urgent warning from Blue Soup 2.0
Do not attempt this diet yourself, particularly if you like going to the toilet more than once a month.

Chapter Four

In which ... oh no, we're not doing that any more.

Icky's herby dumplings really were the best he'd ever made. The three housemates sat back contented and replayed the delicious taste in their minds. For a full half hour there was not a sound to be heard except the tedious squeak of Bryan flossing his teeth.

It was Stinky who finally broke the silence. "Great meal, Icks," he said.

The tedious squeak stopped for a moment. "Yes, thank you, Icky," added Bryan. "I never knew you could cook."

"I couldn't," replied Icky. "Not till today."

"That's odd," said Stinky.

Icky's eyes narrowed. "Something's changed about you, Stinky," he said.

"What, like my pants?" asked Stinky.

"I think it's your eyelashes," replied Icky. "Your eyelashes are longer."

"Yes," said Bryan. "You look kind of ... gentler."

"That's funny," said Stinky. "So do you."

"Shall we wash up now?" asked Icky.

"Wash up?" repeated Stinky. "Do we usually wash up?"

"No," said Icky. "But I think it's time we got this place tidy."

"It is a mess," agreed Bryan. So saying, he jumped up and began picking up various objects and taking them to the bin.

"That's funny," said Icky. "You're walking differently, Bryan."

"In what way?" asked Bryan.

"Usually you march along like a little twit," said Icky. "Now you're kind of ... sashaying."

"*Sashaying?*" repeated Bryan.

"I don't know what it means," said Icky, "but you're definitely doing it."

"Hmm," said Bryan. "I *do* know what it means,

and I'm not generally keen on it."

"Don't throw that rag doll away, Bryan," said Stinky, spotting the object in Bryan's hand, which had come out of a particularly amazing Christmas cracker.

"It's been lying around for ages," said Bryan.

"Yes," said Stinky. "But we've never dressed it up."

"That's an idea!" said Icky. "Let's do that!"

For the moment tidying up was forgotten as the three housemates fussed and fumbled with the rag doll, trying on an oven mitt as a long quilted mermaid party gown, followed by a tea-cloth as an informal wrap-around sarong.

"I don't know why we don't do this more often," said Icky.

"It beats arguing," said Stinky.

"We're just too *competitive*," said Bryan.

"You're right," said Icky. "Things are so much better when we cooperate."

"Icky," said Stinky. "I think the sarong's a little high on the left shoulder."

Icky adjusted it. "Is that better?" he asked.

"Much better," chorused Stinky and Bryan.

The three housemates fell to a long silent ponder, that pleasant kind of ponder you get when your hands and mind are occupied.

"Hey," said Icky, breaking the silence. "Remember the time when Bryan got his head stuck to the door, and we had to cut a hole out of it?"

"What?" said Stinky. "Bryan's head?"

Icky chuckled. "The door!" he cried.

They all laughed, but not in an unkind way.

"I know," said Stinky. "Remember the time when Bryan got his eye stuck to the door, and we were in a raft race, and Bryan went over a weir?"

They laughed again, then a look of concern came over Icky. "It must have really hurt when your eyelashes came off," he said to Bryan.

"It was worth it to see you two happy," replied Bryan.

"That's a nice thought," said Stinky. "Thank you, Bryan."

"I mean it," replied Bryan. "Hey — remember when you saved us from the army of pigs, Stinky?"

"Yeah!" said Stinky. "And remember when we had the best Christmas party in the world ever?"

"Yeah!" said Icky. "And remember when that old man stayed here, with the hideous staring eye, and we murdered him and buried his heart under the floorboards, then started hearing this muffled beating sound which got louder and louder till we couldn't stand it any more and confessed?"

There was a short silence. "Icky," said Bryan gently, "I think that may have been a story you read."

"Oh yeah," said Icky. "Thanks for pointing that out."

The three housemates decided their rag doll was now fit and ready for her fashion parade. They stood her on the table and admired their handiwork.

"What shall we have for tea tomorrow?" asked Bryan.

"How about herby dumplings?" suggested Stinky.

"Frabjous idea, Stinky!" said Icky.

Stinky blushed. "It just came to me," he mumbled.

"We'd better get some more herbs," said Bryan, struggling to his feet.

"I'll help you, Bryan," replied Icky, also rising.

Icky and Bryan made their way down to the Super Safari Lounge, arms linked, chatting and laughing and gossiping. The moment they saw the

houseplant, however, the conversation stopped. The plant had grown a beautiful flower, as bright and yellow as the sun, and if you looked closely at the centre of it, you could make out the shapes of a small herd of cows – exactly like the centre of a malted milk biscuit.

"I'd like to eat that flower," said Bryan.

"So would I," replied Icky.

"Be my guest," said Bryan.

"No, no!" replied Icky. "After you!"

"I won't hear a word if it," said Bryan.

"Bryan," replied Icky, "I insist."

"OK," said Bryan.

Bryan plucked the flower, gave it another sniff, then nibbled daintily round the edge.

"Mm!" he said, then wolfed the rest in one mouthful.

"Time to go, I think," said Icky. "Stinky will be wanting his bed."

"That's true," replied Bryan. "We must think of Stinky."

Bryan began to exit, then paused for thought. "I wonder whatever happened to that seed?" he asked.

"It certainly is a mystery," replied Icky.

Note from Blue Soup 2.0

Sorry, folks – it's another short chapter. I could just put in a time gap and carry on, but as the next thing that happens is very dramatic, I do need to give you the chance to sit down if you're standing up, or put down the tray of crockery if you're carrying one.

Chapter Five

Icky and Stinky sat blearily around Bryan's unfinished model house the next morning, staring blankly at the rag doll beside the front door.

"We ought to throw that thing away," said Stinky.

"Stupid doll," said Icky.

At this point there was a knock on the kitchen door. That was odd.

No one ever knocked on the kitchen door.

"Hello?" said Stinky.

"Ah," said the voice of Bryan. "You're in there."

"And?" said Icky.

"I'm just about to come in," said Bryan, "and when I do, I don't want anybody to laugh."

"Why should we laugh?" asked Stinky, puzzled.

"Because you are immature," replied Bryan, "and it's the kind of thing you would do."

"Just shut up and come in!" said Icky.

There was a short pause, then the door crashed open and Bryan breezed in purposefully, grabbed

 some eggs and slices of bread and threw them into the all-in-one breakfast maker. "*So* much to do today," he muttered. "*So* much to do."

Icky and Stinky were stunned silent. They'd often seen Bryan march in like this in the morning. But they'd never seen him wearing a paisley dress with long wavy hair pulled back behind a kerchief.

"Bryan …" began Icky. "You're a … a … girl!"

"And?" snapped Bryan.

"And … you're a girl!" repeated Icky.

Bryan huffed loudly and put his or her hands on his or her hips. "What, does that make me inferior or something?" he or she rasped.

Note from Blue Soup 2.0

I think we'll stick to 'he' for now, or things could get very tedious.

"No," replied Icky. "Just … female."

Bryan checked his breakfast. "I can't see what the fuss is about," he sniffed.

"It is a bit of a change," said Stinky.

"Nothing wrong with change," muttered Bryan.

"What happened?" asked Icky.

"Nothing *happened*," replied Bryan. "I just woke up and I was a girl, OK? And I had these clothes on, and they won't come off, not that I necessarily *want* them off, except I do, but *they won't come off*, all right?"

Bryan grabbed for his breakfast, forgetting it was scalding hot, and sent the whole lot clattering over the floor. "Darn it!" he cried, blowing on his fingers. "That's another nail gone!"

Stinky did his best to help pick up the breakfast,

but only succeeded in scattering a load of maggots on it. Bryan threw the lot away and sank into a chair in a deep sulk. "Why does everything happen to *me?*" he moaned.

At this, a sudden thought struck Icky. "The flower!" he cried.

"What flower?" asked Stinky.

"Bryan ate the flower!" explained Icky. "The one that grew on the herby houseplant!"

"I only ate it because you told me to,"

mumbled Bryan, not quite honestly.

"I never saw a flower on the herby houseplant," said Stinky.

"It grew while we were having tea," explained Icky.

"That's fast," replied Stinky.

"Hmm," said Icky, thinking about this. "I wonder if the whole thing grew that fast?"

Bryan looked up. "You don't think ..." he began.

"It grew from the seed!" cried Icky, excitedly.

"It grew from the seed!" repeated Bryan, fearfully.

"What seed?" said Stinky.

"This explains everything," said Icky. "The leaves made us stop fighting, then the flower turned Bryan into a girl."

"I don't see the connection," replied Bryan.

"Of course there's a connection!" said Icky. "Girls are warm, loving people who never fight."

"They are?" said Stinky.

"Apparently," said Icky.

Note from Blue Soup 2.0

Icky never had a sister and had actually met very few girls. He had however watched many old cartoons, such as "Thumbelina", "Snow White" and "Cinderella", before the Spoonheads mistook these films for garbage and sent them to the interplanetary dump.

"If it grew from the seed," suggested Bryan, "maybe there is an antidote."

Stinky nodded thoughtfully. He had an Aunty Dot himself, although she was in the space zoo now, along with all the other adults.

"Maybe the antidote grows near it," suggested Icky, "like dock leaves grow near nettles."

"How can anything grow near it?" snapped Bryan. "Stinky planted it in a pot!"

"Maybe the lady could help us," suggested Stinky.

There was a short silence.

"Lady?" repeated Bryan. "What lady?"

"The lady in the attic," replied Stinky. "The one that gave me the seed."

A small but pronounced frown appeared on Bryan's brow. "Stinky," he said, as calmly as possible, "did you not think of telling us about this lady before?"

Stinky scratched his head. "I thought I had told you," he replied.

"No, Stinky," said Bryan. "You did not tell us."

"Sorry," replied Stinky.

"Maybe you'd better tell us about her now," suggested Bryan.

"Well ..." said Stinky, casting his mind back, which wasn't easy, "... she's in a glass cabinet, and she's very pale ... she's got dead flowers in her hair ... she doesn't really talk, just points ... except her fingers have kind of rotted away ... but she does seem quite nice."

"I see," said Bryan. "And this is the lady who gave you the seed, which you planted in the pot, which grew into the plant, which produced the flower that I have now eaten."

"That's right," replied Stinky.

Slowly and dramatically, Bryan lowered his face into one hand, while the other beat slowly and rhythmically against the table. The sound of quiet sobbing filled the air.

"This lady sounds *gonk*!" said Icky. "How did she give you the seed if she was in a cabinet?"

"It was in her hand," replied Stinky. "She

kind of offered it up to me."

"You opened the cabinet?" said Icky, eyes agog.

"Just long enough to get the seed," replied Stinky. "I closed it quick again, cos she was going all green and sticky."

Bryan's sobs grew slightly louder.

"I think we'd better go and see this lady," said Icky.

Chapter Six

It had been quite a while since either Icky or Bryan had been into the Attic of Horrors, and things had obviously changed up there. This may have been because they'd messed around with the control panel, but not necessarily. It was possible the attic changed from time to time anyway, just to keep the housemates on their toes. After all, even the most horrible things can seem normal after a while, once you get used to them.

The new attic looked very old indeed. Dusty antiques were everywhere, most of them glass-fronted cabinets. These cabinets stood, or lay, at odd angles, some empty, some filled with books, or china, or stuffed birds. But in the centre of the room lay one very distinct cabinet, much bigger than the rest and lit by an eerie blue light. Led by Stinky, the three housemates crept up to this cabinet. Just as Stinky had promised, it contained a lady – a pale, pale lady, with dead flowers in her hair and little painted symbols on her cheeks. She wore a kaftan, which (as Bryan knew) was a long, loose Arabic dress, and beside her was a battered old guitar.

"You never told us she had a guitar," said Icky.

"Is that what it is?" said Stinky.

"Were her eyes closed before?" asked Icky.

"No," replied Stinky. "Definitely open."

"Maybe she'd having a nap," suggested Icky.

"Maybe she's gone dead," suggested Stinky.

"She's already dead, isn't she?" muttered Bryan.

Suddenly, without warning, completely out of the blue, the pale lady's eyes shot open. The three housemates leapt back like firecrackers.

"Why does that *always* happen?" complained Icky.

"Poo!" said Bryan. "What's that smell?"

"Must be the rotten liquid going down her arm," said Icky.

"Actually," said Stinky. "I think it's the rotten liquid going down my—"

"Thank you, Stinky, that will do!" barked Bryan.

Summoning up their best courage, the three housemates edged back towards the cabinet. The pale lady's eyes were still open, but stared forward at nothing in particular in a kind of meaningless way.

Bryan decided it was time for someone to take charge, someone called Bryan.

"Now look here!" he boomed. "The seed you gave Stinky turned me into a girl, and I want to go back to how I was *right now*, and you had better bally well tell me how!"

Suddenly the pale lady's eyes locked on to Bryan in a death grip stare which was very meaningful indeed. Soundless words issued from her lips.

"What's she saying?" asked Icky.

"You … are … the … the … *something*," said Bryan.

"You are the something?" repeated Stinky. "What's that supposed to mean?"

"Ssh!" said Bryan. "I'm trying to lip-read!"

The pale lady repeated her soundless sentence, more slowly this time.

"You are the ... the *chosen one*," pronounced Bryan.

"Wow," said Stinky.

"I already knew that," said Bryan.

"Look!" said Icky. "She's pointing!"

The pale lady had indeed lifted her putrid arm and indicated the guitar.

"I think she wants you to take it, Bryan," said Icky.

"I don't want it!" complained Bryan.

"Just take it!" said Icky.

"I'm not opening the cabinet!" said Bryan. "You take it!"

"I'm not the chosen one," replied Icky.

"I'll open the cabinet," offered Stinky, "if Bryan takes the guitar."

Bryan did not look keen.

"You'll be fine, Bry," said Stinky. "I got the seed out of there, and nothing happened to me."

"Things don't happen to you," replied Bryan. "Things happen to me."

"Bryan," said Icky. "It may be your only chance to go back to normal."

"I was never normal," replied Bryan.

"That's true," said Icky.

Icky's words, however, had struck home. Bryan began to prepare himself for a quick strike, like the neck of the cobra or the sticky tongue of the poison frog. He instructed Stinky to take hold of the handle which opened the cabinet, and wait for a count of three.

"One ..." began Bryan.

"Two ..."

"Two-and-a-half ..."

"THREE!"

Stinky ripped open the glass door. Bryan's arm shot inside and grabbed the guitar by the neck. Unfortunately, however, Bryan was not *quite* fast enough. Amazingly, the pale lady's arm moved even faster and grabbed *him* by the neck. Slowly, with incredible force, she drew Bryan's terrified face towards her, until her thin grey-pink lips were almost against his ear. The lips parted, and in a dry, dusty death-rattle voice, she croaked the words REMEMBER ME.

No sooner had these words escaped than a dramatic change overcame the pale lady. The skin on her face and neck began to shrink and darken,

her limbs shrivelled and her eyes globbed out, followed by a seething mass of foul green liquid, which was also bubbling out of various other parts of her body. In no time at all she was nothing but a skaggy old skeleton in a kaftan with a horrible meaningless grin and, thankfully, no grip at all.

Bryan disentangled himself from the remains and staggered shakily backwards, still holding on to the guitar. It was a fair bet that Bryan would indeed remember the pale lady.

"I don't think we should mess around with the control panel again," said Stinky.

"It was a bit vile," agreed Icky.

"Are you all right, Bryan?" asked Stinky, brushing some gunk off his housemate's arm and leaving some family-size lumps of dandruff instead.

"F-f-f-fine," stammered Bryan.

"She was only trying to be friendly," said Stinky.

"W-what am I supposed to do with this?" asked Bryan, scowling at the guitar.

"Play it?" suggested Stinky.

"I can't play the guitar!" moaned Bryan. "I wish it was a violin," he added.

"Can you play the violin?" asked Stinky.

"No," said Bryan. "But I could learn, and then I could play Paganini's Violin Concerto Number 1 in E Flat Major."

"Why don't you learn the guitar?" suggested Stinky.

"Don't be daft," snapped Bryan. "How can I play Paganini's Violin Concerto Number 1 in E Flat Major on a *guitar*?"

"Maybe," said Icky, "if you play the guitar it'll turn you back into a boy."

"Why should it do that?" replied Bryan.

"It's bound to do *something*," said Icky. "Otherwise the lady wouldn't have said you were the Chosen One and given you it."

Bryan looked suspiciously at the guitar. Yes, it probably would do *something*, but with his luck, something awful.

"I'm going to leave it right here," he announced, "and *no one is to touch it on pain of death*."

So saying, Bryan placed the guitar carefully against the side of the pale lady's cabinet. Sitting in this spot, the guitar took on an even more powerful aura, as if all the deep dark dramas of the universe were locked inside it.

"Now let's go downstairs and think of something else," said Bryan.

"OK," said Icky.

Chapter Seven

Icky's bedsheets were a crumpled mess. He'd tossed and turned, turned and tossed, and counted cows till the cows were udderly sick of being counted. But there was no way he was going to sleep. He could have woken Stinky of course, but he wasn't keen on meeting Nigel again, not until all the adventures were over, and there were obviously a lot of adventures still to come.

There was only one thing for it. He would have to go back to the Attic of Horrors and get that guitar.

As he climbed the stairs, Icky did wonder for a brief moment if it really was worth doing this. It wouldn't be at all nice if the Pale Lady's remains leapt out of the cabinet and grabbed him like she'd grabbed Bryan. Or if the dead birds in the other cabinet suddenly came to life and flocked out all over him. As always, however, Icky's curiosity was stronger than his fears.

Icky climbed the ladder to the attic, pushed open the hatch, and pulled himself up inside. Everything looked much the same. The cabinets were there, the birds were there ...

... but the guitar was gone.

"That's *very* strange," thought Icky. He climbed back down the ladder, but was too frustrated to go back to bed, so decided to visit the Time Travel Garage and climb around on the Time Travel Van for a while.

The Time Travel Garage, as you all know, was on the bottom floor of the House of Fun, and as Icky started on the last flight of stairs, he became aware of a strange sound in the air. It was a kind of pinky-dinky sound, a bit like music but not as musical. People who knew about these things, which didn't include Icky, would instantly have recognised the sound of a guitar being played badly.

Icky strained his ears to detect where the strange sound was coming from. He crept towards the kitchen, but the sound got quieter. He opened the door to the cellar, but it wasn't coming from there either. As Icky moved towards the Living Living Room, however, the sound got noticeably louder, and was suddenly joined by a frail, warbly voice.

"Can you feel the wind that's blowing through the air?
A magic wind with flowers in its hair?
That's the wind of love
Of butterflies and doves
And jingle-jangle stardust everywhere."

Icky placed his hand on the door and gently eased it open. The room was lit by a flickering candlelight, and all the furniture had gathered round the sofa.

There on the sofa, as usual, sat the five potatoes which used to be Dronezone and General Pig. Beside them sat Bryan, picking tentatively at the guitar which sat on his knee. At the sight of Icky he stopped, and every one or thing in the room turned towards the open door.

"Hi," said Bryan. "Dronezone were just teaching me the guitar."

"Oh," replied Icky. "I thought I was the only one who could understand them."

"We've made a connection," said Bryan. "Did you hear the song we made up?"

"Was that what it was?" replied Icky.

There was a minuscule squeak from the sofa and Bryan bent his head towards the nearest potato. "Sorry, what was that, Ronan?" he said.

Another tiny squeak.

"OK," said Bryan. "I'll try changing the A major to an A minor. What was A minor again?"

A row of little squeaks was followed by Bryan adjusting his fingers on the guitar and strumming carefully on a chord.

"By the way," said Bryan, indicating Dronezone, "this is Ronan, Vernon, Calum and Spit. Funny we've never got to know their names."

"Hi, boys," said Icky. "Pleased to meet you for the ninety-fifth time."

"We were laughing about that time Spit rolled into the hall," said Bryan.

"Yes, I remember that," replied Icky.

"It's amazing how quickly I've picked up this thing," commented Bryan, giving the guitar another strum.

"It didn't work, then," said Icky.

"What didn't work?" asked Bryan.

"You're still a girl," said Icky.

"Oh yes," said Bryan. He ran his hand down his long and actually quite lovely tresses. "I've been thinking," he added. "There *are* certain advantages to being a girl."

"Such as?" asked Icky.

"Well," replied Bryan. "I'm closer to Sister Moon, for a start."

Icky screwed up his face. "Are you joking?" he asked.

"Joe King?" replied Bryan. "No, I'm Bryony Brain."

Note from Blue Soup 2.0

OK, folks. I think we'd better start using 'she' from now on.

"Now," said Bryony Brain. "How about finishing that song?" She cleared her throat and began another frail warble:

"Can you feel the wind that's blowing through the air?
A magic wind with flowers in its hair?
That's the wind of love
Of butterflies and doves
And jingle-jangle stardust everywhere.

So come and share the gentle people's cake
And in the morning when you reawake
You will feel the wind
Let it out and breathe it in
Love the good vibrations that you make.

Can you smell the wind that shakes my tambourine?
Blowin' through the golden garden wild and green?
Oh catch the wind of love
Of butterflies and doves
That swirling, whirling, curling world of dreams!"

Bryony's warble came to an end and there was a gentle clattering noise from the furniture, which could possibly have been applause.

"Thank you so much, everybody," said Bryony. "But now I really must be getting to bed. Mustn't be late for the peace-copter tomorrow!"

"Peace-copter?" said Icky. "What's a peace-copter?"

70

"I'm not totally sure," replied Bryony. "I only know it's coming."

"How do you know?" asked Icky.

"Female intuition," replied Bryony.

"Hmm," said Icky. "Maybe I should take that guitar away for a while."

A look of utter horror came over Bryony's face. She clutched the guitar to her bosom. "Never!" she cried. "Without this guitar ... I wouldn't know who I was!"

Chapter Eight

Icky, Stinky and Bryony Brain stood on the great flat roof of the House of Fun admiring a view they'd never seen before.

"I never realised the roof was so big," said Icky.

"I never realised there *was* a roof," said Stinky.

Note from Blue Soup 2.0

Some of you clever-clogs out there are probably saying "How can there be a flat roof when there's an attic?" Well, that shows how little you know. According to old Earth dictionaries, an attic is the 'uppermost storey of a house'. It doesn't have to be that bit of spare house between the roof and the ceiling. It could be a room on one corner of the roof.

So, as you Earth children say, nerr.

"You really don't have to come with me, you know," said Bryony. She stood slightly apart from the others, clutching her guitar, with a faraway look in her eyes.

"We want to come," said Icky, which wasn't quite true, because Stinky didn't actually know why they were on the roof. Then again, Icky wasn't entirely sure why they were there either. He just wanted to keep a close eye on Bryony.

Bryony checked her watch. "Should be here by now," she muttered, looking upwards.

Stinky looked down. "Is that a letter we're standing on?" he asked.

"Well done, Stinks," said Icky. "It's the letter H."

"It's a very big letter H," replied Stinky. "What does it stand for?"

Hardly had these words escaped Stinky's lips when a dark shadow overcame the H and a great wind beat down upon the housemates.

"Hallelujah!" cried Bryony. "It is come!"

Icky grabbed Stinky and pulled him to the side of the roof. The two of them cowered together as a great flying whirlybird descended, rotor blades scything the air. But Bryan stood where he was, buffeted by the wind, guitar raised to the sky. The whirlybird squatted within millimetres of him, and as the dust settled, revealed its full beauty. Every bit of it was covered in colourful flowers, except the bits that were covered in hearts and rainbows and strange intriguing symbols.

But the greatest surprise was yet to come. The hatch to the peace-copter slowly opened to reveal

two fully-grown, very hairy grown-ups, all dressed in white. They'd come prepared with smiles, but as they saw the housemates, the smiles faded.

"Children!" cried the less hairy grown-up, who was probably a woman.

"Grown-ups!" cried Icky and Stinky.

"How come?" said the woman.

"How come?" said Icky and Stinky.

"We were expecting Sorrel," said the woman. She seemed quite nervous of the housemates.

Bryony stepped forward, holding out the guitar. "Did Sorrel own this?" she asked.

The woman's face dropped. "What have you done to her?" she cried.

"I'm afraid she's ..." Bryony sought a nice way of putting it, "... passed on."

"Yeah!" said Icky. "She's just a skaggy skeleton now!"

A look of terrible alarm came over the two grown-ups. Then the woman seemed to take stock. Suddenly her face lit up with a strange painted smile. "That's fabulous!" she said. "At last her spirit can be reborn as a lark!"

The man smiled also, at least he seemed to smile, as it was hard to see his

face behind his long ginger dreadlocks. "But who will sing at the Festival Without End?" he asked.

Bryony's voice rang out loud and clear: "I shall sing at the festival."

"You will?" said Stinky.

"I have Taken On The Mantle," declared Bryony. "I am ... the Special One."

The woman was still suspicious. "How do we know?" she asked.

Bryony slung the strap of the guitar over her shoulder, struck a chord, and began her plaintive warble:

"Can you feel the wind that's blowing through the air?
A magic wind with flowers in its hair?
That's the wind of love
Of butterflies and doves
And jingle-jangle stardust everywhere."

Bryony closed her eyes for a moment, then gave the guitar one final emphatic strum.

The two grown-ups seemed entranced.

"It could almost be her," trilled the woman.

"Come," said the man. "You must join us in the peace-copter!"

Bryony made to jump straight aboard, but Icky barred her way. "Hang on, hang on, hang on," he said.

"What's the problem, man?" asked the woman.

"Who *are* you?" ordered Icky. "And how come you're not up in the Space Zoo with all the other grown-ups?"

The woman smiled. "Because we are the Children of Musk," she declared.

"The Spoonheads did visit us," added the man. "But we freaked them out and they left."

"Wow," said Icky. "How did you freak them out?"

"Just by being ourselves," replied the woman.

"I'm Periwinkle, by the way," said the man, "and this is Moon Juice."

"Now you've freaked *me* out," said Icky.

"I'm hopeless with names," said Stinky. "Mind if I call you Perry and Moo?"

The man and woman laughed long and hard, a little too hard in fact. "Perry and Moo it is," said Perry.

"I've forgotten those names now," said Stinky.

Bryony held out her hand. "My name," she said, "is Bryony Brain."

Perry and Moo hesitated, then gave Bryony's hand a quick shake. *"Bryony Brain,"* repeated Perry. *"Bryony ... Brain."*

"I can see that name cut into a crop circle," said Moo.

"Come," said Perry. "Time is passing. We need you on stage before sunset."

Chapter Nine

It certainly was peaceful in the peace-copter, with just the soothing chunter of the rotor-blade, the Earth sweeping gracefully below, and the sound of Icky asking "Are we there yet?" every two minutes.

Perry and Moo still seemed strangely nervous of the housemates. They asked them nicely to stay in their seats, because they didn't believe in telling children what to do, but Icky was not very good at staying in a seat. Icky preferred to hover just behind the pilot's seat, hopping from foot to foot and occasionally tapping Moo on the shoulder as he asked his favourite question.

After an hour or so of this, Perry and Moo were also hoping to get there as soon as possible.

Bryony, on the other hand, was keen to stay in the air as long as she could. That was because Perry and Moo had told her that the audience would be expecting at least thirty-five songs, just like Sorrel used to sing. That meant Bryony had to compose roughly thirty-four more, which wasn't easy when the only title coming into your head was, "Are we there yet?"

"Are you sure I can't do just one song?" she pleaded.

"Sorry, man," replied Moo. "The other singers need a break. Remember, this is the Festival Without End, and some of them have been performing for several years."

"*Why* is it the Festival Without End?" asked Stinky.

"Because the Circle Must Be Unbroken," replied Perry.

"It's only because of the festival," added Moo, "that there is World Peace."

Icky stopped hopping around for a moment, just long enough to go, "Eh?"

"When we sing and dance," explained Moo, "we send out a Love Vibe. That's why there's World Peace."

Icky screwed up his face. "World Peace," he replied, "is because Blue Soup made everyone equal and everything fair and does all the washing-up."

"They just want you to think that, man," replied Perry.

"They've messed with your heads," added Moo.

Icky was not convinced, Bryony was not listening, and Stinky was wondering how they could have made his head any more messy than it already was. In any case, the conversation came to an end when a luminous purple lozenge appeared outside the window.

"Woah!" said Stinky. "What's that?"

"I-I don't know," said Moo. "I-I've never seen anything like it before."

"It's a Spoonhead Spybot," declared Bryony. "Everybody knows that."

It was kind of reassuring that Bryony was still a little bit like Bryan. But it wasn't reassuring the way the purple lozenge kept surging up towards the window and popping like a flash gun. Eventually, however, it had seen all it wanted to see, and vanished as quickly as it had appeared.

"You shouldn't have questioned Blue Soup," said Icky.

"They're just messing with our heads," said Moo.

"They've certainly messed with my pants," said Stinky.

Suddenly there was an excited cry from Perry: "Land ahoy!"

Icky and Stinky rushed to the left-hand window, through which Perry was looking. Below them was a golden beach followed by a lush green forest.

"Wow," said Stinky.

"That's Love Island," said Perry.

"It looks frabjous," said Icky. "What's the other side like?"

Icky sprang over towards the right-hand window, but to his surprise, found Moo barring his way. "You don't want to look out there," she said.

"Why not?" said Icky.

"You'll unbalance the copter," replied Moo.

"Eh?" said Icky. "But I was sat there before!"

"Yes, but we're banking now in order to land," replied Moo.

"Just one look!" said Icky.

"No!" cried Moo. "I mean … it's up to you, man, but I'd rather you didn't, so don't."

There was another cry from Perry. "Look over here, man!" he cried. "The festival!"

Icky darted back over to the left-hand window, where Bryony nervously joined him. Below them a massive brown pyramid was appearing.

"Ducks deluxe!" cried Icky. "What's *that*?"

"That's the stage, man," said Perry.

"It took us two years to make that," pronounced Moo, proudly.

"Out of wicker," added Perry.

Bryony's legs went very watery. Any second now they would see the crowd. Bryony had never been to a festival, but she'd seen pictures of the masses with their tents and their beer and their wild behaviour. It didn't bear thinking about.

However, Bryony was in for a surprise. The crowd, when it appeared, was not that big at all. In fact, it was about twenty people.

"Where's everyone else?" asked Icky.

"Everyone else?" replied Moo. "We're here, of course!"

The peace-copter puttered down towards a corner of the field. The small crowd rushed towards it. Their hair was long, their clothes were white, and they were all as old as Perry and Moo.

"Aren't there any kids?" moaned Icky.

The gentle smile faded from Moo's face. "No," she said, grimly. "There are no kids."

"How come?" asked Icky.

Moo did not reply.

"Hold tight," said Perry. The peace-copter

bumped on to the ground and the engine wound down. The crowd formed an excited semicircle around the exit hatch, but when Icky and Stinky appeared, everybody backed away. Moo had to tell them to remain calm.

"It's cool, everybody!" she cried. "The kids are cool!"

Nobody seemed convinced, possibly because Moo didn't sound convinced herself.

"Where's Sorrel?" somebody cried.

Moo smiled broadly. "Wonderful news, everybody!" she cried. "Sorrel's spirit has moved on … into a nightingale!"

"I thought it was a lark," muttered Icky.

"A lark!" cried Moo. "That's it, a lark!"

There was a stunned silence.

"Behold," cried Moo. "The new Child of Musk!"

Bryony inched shyly into the doorway and raised a half-hearted fist.

The crowd remained unconvinced.

"Do you know your dress is on the wrong way round?" someone cried.

"No," said Bryony. "But if you sing it, I'll try to play it."

Note from Blue Soup 2.0

I'm sorry, everybody. This last exchange never happened. I just want you to realise I'm more humorous than the last Blue Soup. Maybe I'm trying too hard. Let's go back to the real story.

The crowd remained unconvinced.

"How do we know you're not carrying bad karma?" someone cried.

"Can't you see?" replied Bryony. "I'm carrying a guitar."

Suddenly there was a cry from over by the stage. "Rocket's collapsed!"

At this, there was near panic. Rocket had obviously been performing, but all that could be seen of him now was the top of a top hat with a feather sticking out of it. A loud hum came out of the PA speakers, and nothing that sounded like music.

"Quick!" said Moo. "Get Bryony on stage!"

The crowd's doubts were quickly forgotten as Bryony was half hustled, half carried towards the stage. On her way she met Rocket going the other way, semi-conscious on a blanket.

Rocket turned out to be a rather old man, with a deeply-lined face and long wisps of thin grey hair poking out of his feathered hat. "Good luck, man," he groaned.

Bryony's mouth went very dry. When Bryony was Bryan, she had been on stage many times, but that was always to collect prizes, not to sing thirty-five songs she had written half an hour before. She crept up on to the vast podium like a condemned woman climbing on to the scaffold. Shakily she made the long lonely walk to centre stage, perched on a high stool, sat the magic guitar on her knee, and muttered into the microphone.

"Hello, Love Island," she said.

Bryony's voice echoed round the near-empty field like thunder. There was a weak cheer. Bryony began to feel a little more confident.

"How you doin'?" she said.

It quite excited Bryony to drop a 'g' like this, even more so when a stronger cheer came back. A surge of excitement went through her. Maybe she was cut out to be a festival headliner after all.

"Now look here," she said. "I've got some songs I've written, and some of them might not be very good, but I've only been playing one day, so please don't laugh if I get anything wrong."

The atmosphere cooled slightly. Bryony struck a chord on the guitar and weakly crooned the first line of "Can You Feel the Wind?"

The effect was electric. The Children of Musk sat down as one, crossed their legs and began to sway.

It was almost as if Bryony had opened their favourite bedtime story.

"Oh no!" said Icky. "Now he's going to want to be Bryony for ever!"

"What if he just keeps singing, and we can never go home?" asked Stinky.

It was too awful to contemplate. Especially when no one wanted to stand near the housemates, let alone talk to them.

"Let's see if we can make some friends," said Icky.

There were stalls dotted around the edge of the field, which seemed like a good place to start. Icky and Stinky visited the Healing Crystal stall, the Green Lentil Pattie stall, and the Tie-dye T-shirt stall. They tried some idle chatter, some playful joking, and some winning smiles. But the harder they tried, the more the grown-ups seemed to back away. It was as if they carried some horrible disease, which in Stinky's case was possibly true, except the grown-ups had no way of knowing that.

Bryony, on the other hand, was going down great. By the last chorus of "Can You Feel the Wind?" everyone was joining in, and the song ended with a round of applause and a few cheers. Growing in confidence by the second, Bryony launched into her second song, which, coincidentally, had exactly the same words and tune as "Can You Feel the Wind?"

All was not well on the festival field, however. Moo was looking distinctly unhappy. "The festival toilet!" she moaned. "Why has no one emptied it?"

A spotty, curly-headed man hung his head. "Sorry, Moo," he replied. "It was my job, but I just couldn't face it."

"No one can face it, Moo," added a dreadlocked pudgy woman.

Icky turned excitedly to Stinky. "Stinky," he said. "Here's the perfect chance to make ourselves popular!"

"What?" said Stinky. "By emptying the festival toilet?"

"Why not?" said Icky. "I've got no sense of smell, and you're so used to your own smell, you won't notice another one."

"All right then," said Stinky.

Icky strode purposefully forward. "*We'll* do it, Moo!" he exclaimed.

Moo seemed doubtful. "Are you sure?" she asked.

"Course we're sure!" said Icky. "We like cleaning toilets!"

"You haven't seen *these* toilets," replied Moo.

"Pah!" said Icky. "They can't be worse than *our* toilet!"

Icky, however, had spoken too soon. This was, after all, the Festival Without End, and the festival toilet had been used for a very long time, but no one had *quite* got round to emptying it.

Although it stood in the middle of its own special field, in its own special wicker hut, its smell had spread at least as far as the love vibes put out by the Children of Musk.

Moo led the way to this magic hut. As she drew close she took the bandana off her head and tied it around her face. Icky and Stinky pranced along behind her, as happy as sandboys.

"Can't see what the fuss is about," said Icky.

They entered the hut. It really was a medieval scene. To the left were three makeshift bucket-toilets. To the right was some kind of industrial wheely-bin. A pipe like an elephant's trunk came down from there into a dark stinking pit, which lay behind the toilets and the bin and stretched the width of the hut. On the other side of the pit another elephant's trunk emerged and went into a machine like a small old-fashioned train engine.

Moo was keen to get the instructions over as quickly as possible. "Pump cesspit into bin ..." she gasped, "... take bin far away ... empty contents ... bury deep."

Stinky nodded thoughtfully, not having

understood a word. Icky, on the other hand, understood perfectly, which was why one thing was bothering him.

"Why is the pump the other side of the cesspit?" he asked.

"Mistake ..." gasped Moo, "... made cesspit wider ... can't get across ..."

"Is there a ladder to put across?" asked Icky.

"Yes," said Moo.

"Where is it?" asked Icky.

"Other side of cesspit ..." gasped Moo. "... behind pump."

Sure enough, there on the far side of the pit lay a nice long ladder, exactly where it shouldn't have been.

"Good luck," gasped Moo. "Must go now."

Moo departed in great haste, covering her mouth with her hand. She had certainly left the housemates with a conundrum. But Icky was not a person to put off that easily.

"Hmm," he said, studying the cesspit. "I reckon I could jump that."

A flicker of anxiety tickled Stinky's face. "Are you sure, Icky?" he said. "It's very wide."

"I'm brilliant at long jump," said Icky. "I've just got to take a really long run-up, hit the board hard, and do a little hitch-kick at the end."

Icky demonstrated his little hitch kick, then went to the edge of the cesspit and looked over. "I wonder how deep it is?" he asked.

"Dunno," replied Stinky. "Can you swim?"

"I can swim in water," said Icky.

"That's not water," replied Stinky.

"Pah!" said Icky. "I'll be fine!"

Icky began to pace out his run-up, first to the doorway, then out into the field. About fifty metres across, he stopped and made a mark with his heel. At this point he gazed towards the hut and stroked his chin. Then he turned and began pacing out a longer run-up. He made another mark, considered, then paced back some more. Soon he was just a dot on the horizon, then not even that. For a while it seemed he had vanished completely. Then there was a distant cry of "Geronimo!", and a flying dot appeared at the far end of the field. Bit by bit the dot became an Icky, homing in on the cesspit like a rabbit with its tail on fire.

About halfway across the field, however, there were distinct signs that Icky was slowing. By the time he reached the toilet hut, the manic sprint had become a gasping lollop.

"Bail out, Icky!" cried Stinky. "You're not going to make it!"

But nothing could stop Icky now. His eyes were glazed and fixed on the far side of the cesspit. With a last desperate intake of breath he lolloped the final few metres, hit the imaginary board, leapt into the air, and ...

Note from Blue Soup 2.0

I sincerely hope that none of you are hoping Icky doesn't make it. If so, you're not the kind of person we want as a reader, so go and read something nasty like Grimm's Fairy Tales.

... SPLOSH!

Icky stood up and brushed himself down. "Fancy that," he said. "Clear the cesspit then land in a puddle the other side. Lucky it was only water."

"I thought you weren't going to make it, Icky," said Stinky.

"It was the hitch-kick that did it," replied Icky. "Now, how does this pump work?"

In his usual style, Icky pressed everything that

could be pressed, pulled everything that could be pulled, and gave the pump a kick for good measure. There was a little click, a louder BRRRR, then a mighty SHLOBBLE. The elephant's trunk began to pulsate and a great golloping splatter was heard inside the wheely-bin.

"We're in business!" cried Icky.

"I hope you know where the off-switch is," remarked Stinky.

"I'll just pull the pipe off when it's full," said Icky.

"Is that wise?" asked Stinky.

"It'll be fine!" cried Icky.

It certainly was a big job, but the pump worked a treat. As soon as the bin began to overflow, Icky took hold of the pipe at the pump end and prepared to give it an almighty yank.

"One …" he cried. "Two …"

"Are you sure, Icky?" yelled Stinky.

"… THREE!"

Icky flew backwards, the pipe in his hands, and the pump stopped working.

Note from Blue Soup 2.0

If any of you unpleasant readers are still out there,

perhaps you will give up now. Everyone who has read Stinky Finger's House of Fun knows that Icky has a lucky feather, and nothing bad ever happens to him … at least, hardly ever.

"Piece of cake!" cried Icky. He lowered the ladder over the cesspit, clambered on hands and knees over to his companion, and swung the lid on to the industrial-size bin.

"Come on, Stinky," he cried. "Hardest part's over for sure!"

Chapter Ten

No one had told the housemates exactly *where* to empty the bin, and come to that, exactly how. Moo had said to take it far away, however, so they pushed it over several meadows, through a couple of woods, alongside a merry brook, and up a not-so-merry hill. Halfway up this hill they began to hear shrill voices which sounded very excited about something. Icky and Stinky were also excited, because they hadn't realised anyone else was on the island. They heaved the bin to the top of the hill and scanned the scene below.

The scene in question was one of flowery beauty, with a wide sandy bay curving almost into a circle and gentle green mountains guarding the outlet to the sea. The only problem was, there was a war going on in it.

"What *are* they?" gulped Stinky.

"They look like kids," replied Icky, "except even more violent."

It certainly was a brutal scene. Figures in warpaint and rags were thrashing ten bells out of each other, while others smashed their foreheads into piles of slate, slung rocks at seagulls, or blasted driftwood with makeshift flamethrowers.

"Hmm," said Icky. "I wonder if this is what we weren't supposed to see out of the copter?"

"Get down, Icky!" cried Stinky. "They've seen us!"

It was too late. A group of girls had stopped thrashing each other with tea-trays and were staring straight at the housemates. One especially wild girl screamed at everybody else to pay attention.

"Strangers!" she cried.

Every pair of eyes fixed on Icky and Stinky. Every pair of hands raised a weapon.

"What are you?" yelled Wild Girl.

Icky, as usual, knew no fear. "What do we look like?" he cried.

101

"A pair of morons!" yelled Wild Girl.

The wild kids laughed.

"Yeah, well you look like …" Icky desperately wanted to say something clever, but nothing would come. "… a load of funny people!"

The wild kids laughed again. Wild Girl's eyes focused on the large object beside Icky and Stinky. "What's in that bin?" she bawled.

"Nothing much," yelled Icky.

"Think we're stupid?" bawled Wild Girl. "You wouldn't be pushing a bin full of nothing much!"

"It's treasure!" someone else shouted.

"Is it treasure?" yelled Wild Girl.

"Kind of," replied Icky.

"In that case," yelled Wild Girl, "it's ours."

As one, the wild kids began to advance up the hill.

"Wait!" cried Icky. "You don't want this!"

"Don't tell us what we want!" cried Wild Girl.

"Honest!" yelled Icky. "It's full of …" He turned to Stinky. "What was that long word they taught us in school?" he asked. "The one it's all right to use?"

"Dictionary?" replied Stinky. It was the longest word he knew.

"No, the word for this!" said Icky. "Ex …
something."

"Excalibur?" suggested Stinky.

"Excitement!" said Icky. "That's it, excitement!"
He cupped both hands round his mouth and yelled
down the hill: "It's full of excitement!"

With a great roar the wild kids raised their
weapons and charged. Icky and Stinky were left
with no option but to defend themselves the only
way they could. With a mighty heave they sent the
refuse bin bumping and clattering down the hill.
Just short of the wild kids it struck a rock, teetered,
then slammed down on its side, sending

XXXXXXXXXXXXXXXXXXXXXXXXXXXX
XXXXXXXXXXXXXXXXXXXXXXXXXXXX
XXXXXXXXXXXXXXXXXXXXXXXXXXXX
XXXXXXXXXXXXXXXXXXXXXXXXXXXX
XXXXXXXXXXXXXXXXXXXXXXXXXXXX
XXXXXXXXXXXXXXXXXXXXXXXXXXXX
XXXXXXXXXXXXXXXXXXXXXXXXXXXX
XXXXXXXXXXXXXXXXXXXXXXXXXXXX
XXXXXXXXXXXXXXXXXXXXXXXXXXXX
XXXXXXXXXXXXXXXXXXXXXXXXXXXX
XXX

Note from Blue Soup 2.0

For legal reasons I am now required to include the following statement:

The Cosmic Bedtime Children's Book Censors Board (CB^3) has removed three lines from the story 'Peace and Love at the House of Fun'.

The three lines were in breach of regulation 53b, subsection 12 ('Unacceptable Toilet Humour').

Varg Snarpgurgle, Secretary, ICBCB.

Now on with the story.

Icky and Stinky viewed the scene of devastation below and winced. Wild Girl was drawing herself up to her full height of 1m 22 cm and there was thunder in her eyes.

"We know where you come from!" she stormed. "Go back there now ... and tell them we are at war!"

Chapter Eleven

Icky and Stinky arrived breathless back at the festival field. "War!" they cried. "Get weapons, everybody! We're at war!"

Perry hushed the flustered housemates. "Cool it, man," he said. "This is a festival of Peace."

"Not any more!" blurted Icky. "There's these kids on the island, see, and they're mentalists! They've got flamethrowers, and they're coming to get us!"

Moo joined Perry. She wore a frown. "You're talking," she said, "about our children."

"The Children of the Children of Musk," explained Perry.

"They're *your children?*" gasped Icky. "What went wrong?"

"They just got into a bad vibe," said Moo.

105

"We gave them everything," added Perry. "Everything they wanted. We didn't want to be heavy parents, so we let them do whatever they wanted."

"What if they wanted to hit you in the face?" asked Stinky.

"They did," replied Perry.

"What did you do?" asked Icky.

"We said, 'I don't agree with what you've just done'," explained Moo, "'but I recognise your right to do it'."

"I can't understand what went wrong with them," said Perry.

Icky glanced anxiously at the horizon. "The fact is," he said, "they're coming, and we better do something quick!"

"OK," said Moo. "It's cool."

"It is?" said Stinky.

"We'll get everyone into a circle," said Moo.

"What, like a wagon train?" said Icky.

"Not exactly like a wagon train, no," replied Moo.

"What about a square?" suggested Icky. "Then, when the front line get shot, the second line just step over them and carry on firing."

"The purpose of the circle," pronounced Moo, carefully ignoring Icky, "is to hold hands and chant."

"Hold hands and chant?" snorted Icky. "What good's that going to do?"

"It will bring on Good Karma," explained Perry.

"Can he fight?" asked Stinky.

"You're not quite digging my meaning," replied Perry.

"What if one of the wild kids hits someone over the head with a spade?" asked Icky. "What do we do then?"

"That's simple," replied Moo. "The people on either side move together and complete the circle again."

"But what if everyone gets hit over the head with a spade?" asked Icky.

"Then we will have a Moral Victory," declared Moo.

"What's a Moral Victory?" asked Stinky.

"We will all be dead," replied Moo, "but we will have kept our principles."

Icky frowned hard. "I don't like the sound of this

Moral Victory," he said. "It sounds a lot like losing."

"Come!" cried Moo, ignoring Icky again. "Let us make the circle now!"

It wasn't an easy job. Some of the Children of Musk had problems standing up straight, let alone forming a circle. Eventually, however, they all managed to get it together – all, that is, except Bryony, who gamely kept the festival going with her ninety-third song, which sounded suspiciously like her first.

The circle had formed just in time. A horrible shriek arose from the toilet field, and the Wild Kids appeared in the distance, moving forward in a menacing pack.

"I hope they've had a wash," said Icky.

"Let the chant begin!" cried Moo.

There was a low OMMMMM, followed by a louder TAMA-LAMA, pursued by a rhythmic BAH! BAH! BAH! It did nothing to put off the Wild Kids, who were now at the very edge of the festival field and preparing their flamethrowers.

Suddenly there was an almighty WOOOF! A sheet of flame shot across the field and Icky smelled a strange hot plastic stink.

"My shoes are on fire!" he yelled. "My shoes are on fire!"

Icky went into a frantic wardance, running on the spot and flapping at his smouldering feet.

"You've broken the circle!" cried Moo.

"Chant louder, everybody!" cried Perry.

"Get back in the circle!" cried Moo.

"My shoes are on fire!" cried Icky.

The noise was rising to a crescendo. Icky yelped, Bryony warbled, the Children of Musk chanted, and there was a bloodcurdling shriek as the Wild Kids stampeded into the field, smashing up the Tie-dye T-shirt stall and cremating the lentil patties. But just as the battle was about to begin, a new noise arose, a mighty roar which dwarfed all other sounds and brought the Wild Kids to a sudden standstill. All at once the sky became as dark as night, birds fled to their nesting sites, and the very Earth seemed to tremble.

Everybody looked up. As they did so, columns of blue light shot down from above and locked on to the Children of Musk. The roar gave way to a new noise, a cosmic-vacuum-cleaner-type noise, and as one the baffled grown-ups began to rise into the air.

"We're going to Nirvana!" cried Moo.

"Actually," muttered Icky, "I think you're going to the space zoo."

Icky, of course, was quite correct. Like almost everybody on Earth, he'd seen the Spoonheads arrive before in their massive spacecrafts bigger than the sky. He'd seen the grown-ups rise to the heavens, just like the grown-ups now, never to be seen again. But he'd never seen any of them look as happy about it as the Children of Musk.

"Keep on truckin'!" cried Perry, but it was a very small, distant cry, and not long after, the blue beams shrank back up into the mighty spacecraft and it shot away at the speed of light.

For a while there was a stunned silence, even from Bryony. Then Icky and Stinky remembered they were in the middle of a war, and unfortunately so did the Wild Kids. Icky and Stinky made a tactical retreat, at full speed, towards the stage. The Wild Kids pursued them, hacking down everything in their path. Bryony nervously began another verse of "If You're Coming To The House of Fun".

It was a dire situation. Icky and Stinky didn't even have a pointed stick to defend themselves with. Not knowing where else to go, they climbed up on to the stage and looked around desperately for a weapon.

"Bad move, boys!" yelled Wild Girl. "You've got nowhere left to run!"

So saying, Wild Girl led the rest of the Wild Kids up on to the stage, kicking over amps and speakers and turning Bryony's voice into a whisper. Icky and Stinky backed towards Bryony, who seemed to shrink down behind her guitar as if this could give her protection.

Suddenly Icky had an idea. He seized the guitar.

"No!" cried Bryony. "Not the guitar!"

Icky held the guitar before him and advanced towards Wild Girl.

"What are you going to do with that?" sneered Wild Girl. "Play me a song?"

Icky handed the guitar to Wild Girl. "No," he said. "You are."

Wild Girl gave a roar of laughter, narrowed her eyes and raised the guitar like an axe. "Prepare to meet your maker!" she cried.

There was a pause. The axe did not come down. Wild Girl's face was slowly changing, from anger, to confusion, to the mild smile of a nursery teacher. She lowered the guitar slowly, running her eyes lovingly over it as she did so. Then she sat cross-legged on the floor, propped the guitar on her lap, strummed a chord, and began to sing:

"When I get some wicker
I'll make a wicker table
I'll make a wicker handbag

And a little wicker stool
I'll make a wicker fireplace!
I'll put some wicker on it!
I'll burn away the hatred and the anger
Then we'll live in a gentle wicker world!"

The rest of the Wild Kids really didn't know what to make of this. They were obviously itching to get on with smashing things up, but Wild Girl was their leader, and they were trained to obey her. One by one, they took their places around her, nodding thoughtfully or clapping gently in time. Icky and Stinky, just as thoughtfully, found a box of percussion instruments and began handing them out. Soon Wild Girl had a tasteful accompaniment of maracas, bongos, triangles, salt-shakers and spoons. Icky and Stinky were happily losing themselves in the rhythm when they heard a familiar voice behind them: "Can we go now?"

The housemates turned to see Bryan standing self-consciously in a string vest and paisley boxer shorts.

"Hi, Bry!" said Icky.

"Good to have you back," said Stinky.

"Back?" said Bryan. "I've been here all along."

"You could do with some trousers," said Icky.

Bryan looked down, gasped, and wrapped his arms around himself. "Oh no!" he said. "It's that dream again!"

Note from Blue Soup 2.0
If you don't understand this, you haven't read enough House of Fun books.

"Come on, Bry," said Stinky. "We'll get you home."

"Good," said Bryan. "Er ... how, exactly?"

"In the peace-copter, of course!" said Icky. "Let's face it, the Children of Musk won't be needing it."

"That's true," said Stinky. "But how will we drive it?"

"There's bound to be a manual in the glove compartment," replied Icky.

"I shall take charge of that," said Bryan, who was clearly back to his normal self.

"OK, folks!" said Icky, addressing the Wild Kids. "See you around!"

"Peace, man," a few kids replied.

"Sorry about covering you in excitement," said Stinky.

"No problem, man," replied another kid. He held out his hand for the housemates to shake, but Icky and Stinky decided a wave would do nicely.

Chapter Twelve

Bryan studied the model of the model of the model of the model of the model of the House of Fun, sat back and folded his arms. "I think I'll leave it at that," he said.

"It's still not perfect," said Icky.

"No," replied Bryan. "But it doesn't seem to matter any more."

"You'll need to put a peace-copter on the roof," said Stinky.

"I'll do that, by and by," said Bryan, "but for now, I'm just going to chill out."

"Wow," said Stinky. "I can't imagine you chilling out, Bryan."

"Oh, I'm pretty chilled out now," said Bryan. "I think it's the knitting."

Icky and Stinky said nothing. It was better that way. A look of concern came over Bryan. "How are your feet, Icky?" he asked.

"Oh, not so bad, thanks," said Icky. "I popped the blisters, and now they're just like two big slabs of meat with no feeling."

Bryan smiled warmly. "That's good," he said, "I think."

"Well," said Stinky, "I suppose we'd better be getting to bed."

"It's been a long day," said Bryan, "although I can't actually remember what happened in it."

"Night then," said Icky.

"Night," said Stinky.

"Night," said Bryan.

Icky watched his two housemates slope off towards their rooms, but made no move himself. Icky had a fate he could not avoid, a date with destiny, or to be more accurate, a date with Nigel.

As soon as the house was quiet he made his way to the Uninvited Guest Bedroom, put on the jim-jams and dressing-gown he'd left there, and with considerable skill, tied himself up.

All was quiet. The room showed no signs of having been stayed in. The little soaps were still in their wrappers by the sink, and the little milk pots remained unopened by the kettle.

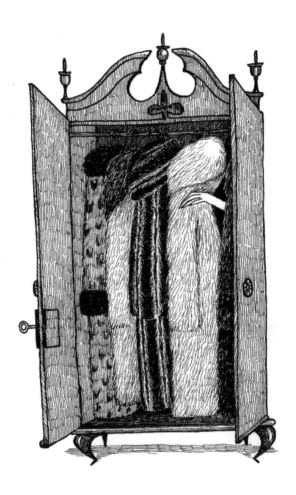

But just as Icky was beginning to think it had all been a dream, there was a cavernous groan from the wardrobe. The wardrobe door flew open to reveal a row of furry coats, one of them grasped by a bony hand. This hand pulled the coats aside, and there, in all his ugly glory, stood Nigel. He stepped out into the room, still with one hand carefully concealed behind his back.

"Iqbal," he said. "So good to see you again."

It worried Icky to be called by his real name, especially by somebody who didn't have a real name of their own. But he gave a big confident smile all the same. "How's it going?" he trilled.

"Adequately," replied Nigel, moving closer.

"How's Jimmy?" asked Icky.

"Hungry," replied Nigel.

"New sandals?" asked Icky.

"Enough of the small talk," replied Nigel.

Nigel was now eye to eye with Icky. He really had quite peculiar eyes, pale grey in colour – all of them, that is, not just the irises.

"And now," he said, "It is time to Relieve the Suspense."

Nigel's arm began to move out from behind his back, very, very slowly, much slower than a tortoise, quite a bit slower than a snail, even slower than a sloth on a bad day.

"One last guess as to what I've got here?" he asked.

"A dentist's drill?" asked Icky.

"Not that," replied Nigel.

"Your old sandals?" suggested Icky.

"Not them either," replied Nigel.

"A CD by Westlife?" asked Icky.

"Never heard of them," replied Nigel.

"I give up," replied Icky.

"Then behold ..." pronounced Nigel, "... the ultimate nightmare!"

With the flourish of a master conjurer, Nigel unveiled a quite magnificent multicoloured feather duster.

"Er ... are you going to do some cleaning?" asked Icky.

"You won't be laughing soon," replied Nigel. So saying, he lowered the feather duster to the level of Icky's feet. "No one, but no one, can bear this duster!" he crowed.

Nigel flickered the duster lightly over the soles of Icky's feet.

Icky was completely unmoved.

Nigel flickered again, a little lighter this time.

Icky shrugged.

Nigel frowned. "You're a very good actor!" he snapped.

"Thank you," replied Icky, "but I'm not acting."

Nigel worked the duster right, left, up, down, slow, quick, hard, soft ... still Icky did not so much as bat an eyelid. Nigel's face darkened to a sunset purple and the vein on his temple bulged like a coiled rope. Eventually he could stand no more. He slammed the duster to the ground, stamped his sandalled foot, and cried, "Curse you, you ... demon!"

"Thank you again," replied Icky.

Nigel stormed over to the wardrobe and yanked out his suitcase. "I'd just like to say," he stormed, "that this guest house is the worst I've ever stayed in. Not only the worst, but also the smelliest."

"I wouldn't know," replied Icky. "I've got no sense of smell."

"No sense of smell … no feeling in your feet …" snarled Nigel. "What kind of freak are you?"

"Just an Icky Bats," replied Icky. "Would you mind signing the visitors' book as you leave?"

With a snarl that could be heard all the way to Love Island, Nigel wrenched open the doors to the Ghost Metro, and was gone, almost certainly for ever, unless he got lost on the way out of the House of Fun, which was always possible.

With a contented hum, Icky drew the lucky feather from his pocket. "You did it again, lucky feather," he said, "although that flamethrower did help." Then he untied himself, padded off to his room on his numb feet, and climbed beneath the cosy covers. How great it was, he thought, that good things could come out of the worst situations. And how great it was not to have to worry about investigating a seed, or a guitar, or anything at all that could disturb a good night's sleep. In no time at all Icky was snoring like a buzz-saw, dreaming of peace, love, and yet more amazing adventures in the House of Fun.

More adventures with Stinky and friends!

STINKY FINGER'S HOUSE OF FUN

Jon Blake

The Spoonheads have arrived in their space-hoovers and sucked up all the grown-ups! So Stinky and Icky will never have to change their underwear again.

In search of an Aim in Life, the two great mates head off to Uncle Nero's House of Fun. But soon they're being besieged by an army of pigs who want to make people pies!

They're going to need more than Icky's lucky feather and Stinky's smelly pants to save their crazy new home ...

More adventures with Stinky and friends!

STINKY FINGER'S CRAZY PARTY

Jon Blake

The Spoonheads have sucked up all the grown-ups into their space zoo, so Stinky and Icky decide to invite all their friends to the greatest party ever.

But disaster strikes during a routine visit to the Brain Drain (to donate brains). Stinky and Icky lose a vital part of their memory! As party-time ticks ever closer, Stinky has to chase the Brain Drain van all the way to Planet Honk to get back their lost minds ...

Another title from Hodder Children's Books:

THE DEADLY SECRET OF DOROTHY W.

Jon Blake

When Jasmin wins a place at the Dorothy Wordsearch School for Gifted Young Writers, things look fishy. Who exactly is the mysterious Mr Collins?

How come Miss Birdshot, the wizened old housekeeper, is so incredibly strong?

And why do Jasmin's fellow pupils keep disappearing?

As Jasmin unravels Dorothy W.'s deadly secret, she finds herself literally writing for her life. Now, only the most brilliant story will help her survive!

'It's original and witty, full of amusing characterisation – a funny adventure story which credits its readers with intelligence.' Books for Keeps

Another title from Hodder Children's Books:

THE MAD MISSION OF JASMIN J.

Jon Blake

The last time Jasmin saw Dorothy Wordsearch, the awful author was being eaten by a monster.

So how come she's still writing stories?

It's time for Jasmin to investigate – helped, but mainly hindered, by her hyper sidekick Kevin Shilling.

And when Kevin is won over by a sinister new enemy, Jasmin will need all her wits to save him from a terrible fate …